THE STUPIDS DIE

Story by Harry Allard
Pictures by James Marshall

Houghton Mifflin Company   Boston

Also by Harry Allard and James Marshall

The Stupids Step Out
Miss Nelson is Missing!
The Stupids Have a Ball

Library of Congress Cataloging in Publication Data

Allard, Harry.
    The Stupids die.

    SUMMARY: The Stupid family think they are dead
when the lights go out.
    [1. Humorous stories] I. Marshall, James,
1942-   joint author. II. Title.
PZ7.A413So   [E]   80-27103
ISBN 0-395-30347-8

Text Copyright © 1981 by Harry Allard
Illustrations Copyright © 1981 by James Marshall

Printed in the United States of America
WOZ 20 19 18 17 16 15

For Chuck Gerhardt and Otto Coontz

One morning Stanley Q. Stupid woke up with a funny feeling.

"Something really stupid is going to happen today," he said.

"Oh, wow!" said the two Stupid kids.

The Stupids all had breakfast in the shower, as usual.

"My eggs are all runny," said Mr. Stupid.

After breakfast the two Stupid kids had chores to do.

Buster mowed the rug.

And Petunia watered all the houseplants.

Bong Bong Bong Bong Bong Bong
Bong Bong Bong Bong Bong
The clock in the hall struck eleven.
"Noon!" cried Mr. Stupid.
"Time for lunch!"

"Buster is eating with his feet," said Petunia.
"By golly," said Mr. Stupid. "Buster has finally learned some manners."

After lunch Mrs. Stupid made a new dress.

"I hope it isn't too loud," she said.

"It's very pretty," said Mr. Stupid.

"Cluck, cluck, cluck," said the dress.

That evening while the Stupids were watching television . . .

. . . everything went dark.

"I can't see a thing," said Mrs. Stupid.

"We must be dead," said Mr. Stupid.

"Oh, wow!" said the two Stupid kids.

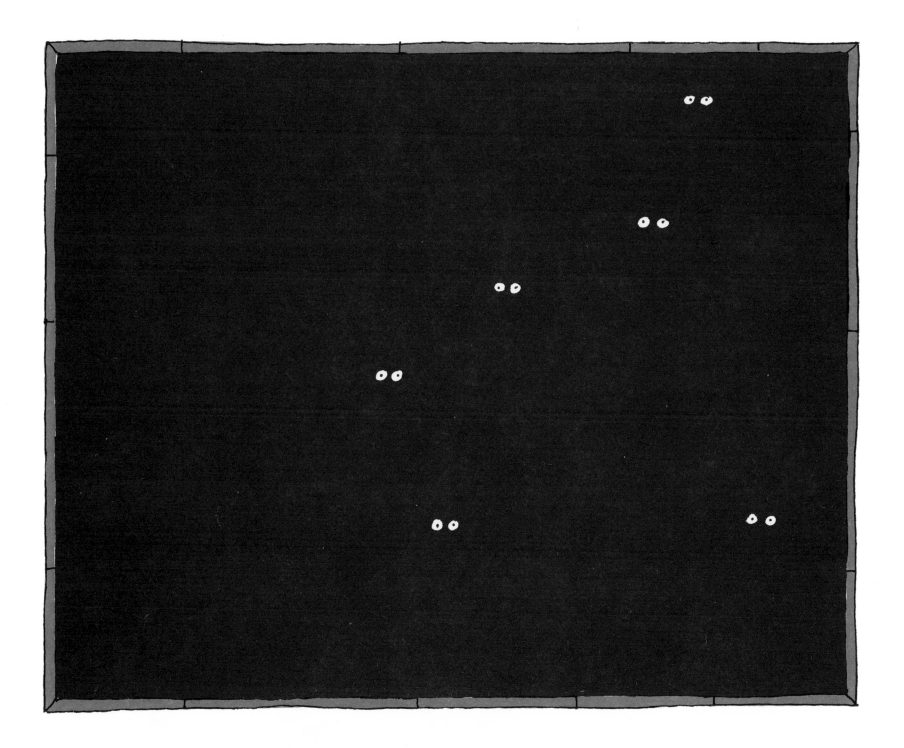

Meanwhile, the Stupids' wonderful dog Kitty and their swell cat Xylophone went to the basement.

The Stupids all looked around.

"This must be heaven," said Mr. Stupid.

"Oh, wow!" said the two Stupid kids.

"It has a nice homey feeling," said Mrs. Stupid.

Just then Grandfather Stupid stopped by.

"Welcome to heaven," said Mr. Stupid.

"This isn't heaven," said Grandfather.

"This is Cleveland."

"This may sound stupid," said Buster.

"But I think this is our living room."

"Oh, heck," said Petunia, "I'm going to bed."

And she put on her sneakers.

"Good night, dear," said Mrs. Stupid.
"I'm sorry nothing really stupid happened
today," said Mr. Stupid. "But we had fun anyway.
We always do."